To the small ones

First U.S. edition 2009

Library of Congress Cataloging-in-Publication Data is available.

Library of Congress Catalog Card Number 2008935657

ISBN 978-0-7636-4275-4

10 9 8 7 6 5 4 3 2

Printed in China

This book was typeset in ITC Bookman.
The illustrations were done in mixed media.

Candlewick Press
99 Dover Street
Somerville, Massachusetts 02144

visit us at www.candlcwick.com

IT'S A SECRET!

JOHN BURNINGHAM

CANDLEWICK PRESS

In Marie Elaine's house

they had a cat whose name was Malcolm.

Every night Malcolm went out, and every morning he came back in. During the day Malcolm slept a lot of the time.

"Where do cats go at night?" Marie Elaine asked.

"I don't know," said Marie Elaine's mother.

"They just go outside somewhere."

One evening in the summer, Marie Elaine came down to the kitchen to get a cold drink from the fridge.

There, by the cat door, was Malcolm the cat, and he was all dressed up in fancy clothes and a hat.

"Why are you all dressed up like that, and where are you going?" asked Marie Elaine.

"I'm going to a party," said Malcolm, "but I can't say where because it's a secret."

"Oh, please, please let me come with you. I'll keep your secret. Please, please let me come," said Marie Elaine.

Malcolm thought for a moment and then said, "All right, but you can't come like that. You'll have to put on something that's right for a party."

Marie Elaine raced up to her room and put on her party dress.

"That's all right, I suppose," said Malcolm, "but you'll have to get small."

Marie Elaine got small, and they went out of the house through the cat door.

Now, little Norman Kowalski was not asleep.
He was looking out the window and saw
Marie Elaine and Malcolm.

"I see you," said Norman. "Where are you
going, and why are you small?"

"We're going to a party and, anyway, it's a secret," said Marie Elaine.

"Let me come," said Norman, "or I'll tell."

"Oh, all right then," said Malcolm, "but you must hurry. The party is starting soon, and we have to get past the dogs."

They rounded the corner, and suddenly
the dogs started to chase them.
They ran as fast as they could and
just managed to get to a fire escape.
They rushed up the stairs, and although
the dogs came after them . . .

Malcolm knew a way where the dogs wouldn't follow.

Finally they arrived at the place
on the rooftops where the party
was about to start.

There were lots and lots of cats,
and some had come from a long
way away.

The cats were very friendly to Marie Elaine and Norman.

They danced with them and let them join in their party games.

Suddenly all the cats became quiet.
All you could hear was them whispering,
"She's coming. She's coming."

It was the Queen of the Cats.

Then they had a delicious midnight feast.

After the feast, the Queen gave
everyone presents to take home.
Marie Elaine was given a little doll,
which was a kitten, and Norman
was given a toy mouse.

Suddenly the Queen said, "Look at the time. The party must end—it will be light soon."

Nobody wanted the party to end; no one wanted to go home.

But the cats all waved good-bye
and set off in different directions.

Malcolm showed Marie Elaine and Norman
the way back home over the rooftops.

"When we go down the fire escape,
we must be very quiet because of the dogs,"
Malcolm said.

They went very quietly past the dogs,
who were asleep.

Then they hurried home as fast as they
could go.

When Marie Elaine got back to her house,
she was very tired and fell asleep on the sofa.

In the morning, her mother was
surprised to see her downstairs.
"You look as if you were out
all night with the cat," she said.
"I was," said Marie Elaine, "and
now I know where he goes at night.
But I can't tell you because
it's a secret."

ML   10
              09